I AM READING

Just Mabel

D1422095

FRIEDA WISHINSKY

Illustrated by

SUE HEAP

KINGFISHER

For my friend Dorothy Joan Harris – F.W.
For Suzanne – S.H.

KINGFISHER
An imprint of Kingfisher Publications Plc
New Penderel House, 283-288 High Holborn
London WC1V 7HZ
www.kingfisherpub.com

First published by Kingfisher 2001
This edition published by Kingfisher 2008
2 4 6 8 10 9 7 5 3 1

A CIP catalogue record for this book
is available from the British Library

ISBN 978 0 7534 1690 7

Printed in China
1TR/1007/WKT/(SCHOY)/115MA

Contents

Just Mabel

Mabel loved to sing.

She sang in the kitchen.

She sang to
the dog.

She sang in the bath.

She even sang in the school
playground.

"When I grow up I'm going to
be a famous singer," said Mabel.

"You'll never be famous with a
plain name like Mabel," said John.

"Mabel is boring."

Mabel stopped singing.

At home that evening, Mabel

wondered if John was right.

What if Mabel *was* boring?

What if she'd never be a famous singer

with a name like Mabel?

Maybe she should change her name?

"Please don't call me Mabel," Mabel
told her parents at dinner that night.
"Call me Holly instead."
"But Holly is your best
friend's name," said
Mabel's mum.
"I know," said Mabel,
"and isn't it beautiful!"

"Mabel is beautiful, too,"
said her dad.

"Not to me," said Mabel.

So Mabel's parents sighed
and agreed to call her Holly.

The next day at school, Mrs Hill called the register.

"Paul," said Mrs Hill.

"Yes," said Paul.

"Emma," said Mrs Hill.

"Yes," said Emma.

"Holly," said Mrs Hill.

"Yes," said Holly.

"Yes," said Mabel.

"You're not Holly. You're Mabel,"
said Mrs Hill.

"Not any more," said Mabel.

"I've changed my name."

"But Mabel is a beautiful name,"
said Mrs Hill.

"Not to me," said Mabel.

"Holly is better."

"But Holly is *my* name," said Holly.

"Anyway there's nothing wrong
with Mabel. Mabel is pretty."

"Not to me," said Mabel, "but I
promise I won't call myself Holly."

Mabel thought and thought.

What name could she use?

What name was beautiful?

At home after school, she found
a postcard on the hall table.
It was from her favourite
aunt – Aunt Marietta.
Yes! That was it!
Marietta was a beautiful name.

Dear Mabel
India is my
kind of place.
Love it!
Love to you
Aunt Marietta
x x x x x x

Address
Holyholm
Lammas
Lane
U.K.

Next day, she told the class, "Call me Marietta."

"Marietta is hard to say," said Holly. And it was.

"Maralella?" said John.

"Marabella?" said Emma.

"Maranetta?" said Paul.

All morning, everyone got it wrong.
Soon Mabel knew she had
to find an easier name.

At breaktime, she found one outside.

"Lily!" she exclaimed. "Lily is short. Lily is easy. Lily is beautiful. Lily is the perfect name for a famous singer!"

"Lily is silly," said John.

"Lily is smelly," said Emma.

"Lily has bugs," said Paul, and he dangled a fat one in front of Mabel's nose.

Mabel flung it away.

"I'm not going to be Lily any more," she told them.

"So now you're nobody?" said John.

"I'm not nobody!" said Mabel.

"One day I'm going to be a famous singer."

But suddenly Mabel *felt* like nobody.

She felt miserable.

She felt so miserable she wanted to

go home . . .

But there were still two long hours
before the end of school.

Finally, the last bell rang.

Mabel trudged home.

She slumped on a chair in the living-room. "What if I never find a good name?" she thought. "What if I'm stuck with Mabel forever?" Mabel sighed.

Then she clicked on the TV.

A man was talking.

"Ladies and gentlemen," he said,

"today I am delighted to

introduce the lovely . . .

the charming . . .

the world-famous . . .

Dame Mabel!"

A tall, graceful woman swept onto
the stage and began to sing.
She had a lovely, lilting
voice, and when she
had finished her song
the audience burst
into applause.

Mabel couldn't believe it. A famous

singer was taking a bow on TV –

and her name was *Mabel*!

"That was fantastic, Dame Mabel,"

said the presenter.

"Please, just call me Mabel,"

said Dame Mabel, smiling.

"This is amazing!" exclaimed Mabel.

"This is wonderful!

That famous singer likes her name.

That famous singer makes Mabel

sound *beautiful*!"

Mabel ran to the hall mirror.

"Mabel," she whispered.

"Mabel," she said louder.

"Mabel! Mabel! Mabel!" she sang,

and soon her name sounded as

lovely as music.

Just then, her mum walked in

from the garden.

"Hello, Holly!" she said.

"I'm not Holly," said Mabel.

"What's your name then?"
asked her mum.

"Don't you know, Mum?"
laughed Mabel. "I'm Mabel –
just Mabel – and I love my name."

"So do I," said her mum, giving
Mabel a hug. "And I love you."

The Red Dress

More than anything, Mabel wanted
a red dress.
She loved red.
Red made her
feel like a
dancer leaping
in air.

Red made her feel like a
queen leading a procession.

Red made her feel like a
star singing on stage.

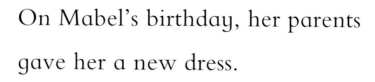

On Mabel's birthday, her parents
gave her a new dress.
The dress was as soft as velvet.
The dress had silver buttons that
shimmered like stars.
The dress was as red as
a sparkling ruby.

"I love my red dress," said Mabel,
hugging her parents. "It's the most
beautiful dress in the world!"

The next day, Mabel skipped all the
way to school in her new red dress.
Mabel saw her best friend Holly.
"I like your new dress," said Holly.

But not everyone agreed.

"You look like a traffic light," said John.

"You look like a fire engine," said Emma.

"You look like a tomato!" said Paul.

"Don't let them bother you, Mabel," said Holly. "Your dress is pretty." Mabel tried not to let them bother her, but she couldn't help it.

Soon Mabel
wished she
wasn't wearing
a red dress.

Soon Mabel
wished she
could hide
her red dress.

Soon Mabel
wished she
didn't *own*
a red dress.

After school, Mabel flung off her red
dress and stuffed it under her bed.
"I'm never wearing *that* again,"
she declared.

The next morning at school, Holly
walked into the classroom with a
new short haircut.

"I like your haircut, Holly,"
said Mabel.

But not everyone agreed.
"Holly looks like
a scarecrow,"
said John.

"Holly looks like a
boiled egg,"said Emma.

"Holly looks like
a bald man," said Paul.

Holly's eyes filled with tears.

Mabel put her arm around her friend.

"Those three are so mean," thought
Mabel. "They're so mean to Holly,
just like . . . just like they were mean
to me about my red dress!"

Mabel glared at John, Paul and Emma.

"Leave Holly alone," she told them.

"We don't have to," said John.

"You can't make us," said Paul.

"We won't," said Emma.

John, Paul and Emma laughed and laughed.

"I wish I could grow my hair back right this minute," Holly sobbed. "Maybe they're right. Maybe I look ugly."

"They're *not* right," said Mabel. "They're not right about anything. They were mean to me yesterday about my red dress. Now they're being mean to you about your hair. But they're wrong, and we can't let them bother us."

"I know," said Holly. "But they *do*."

"Not if we
don't let them,"
said Mabel.
"Not if we stick
together and
have a plan."

Holly wiped her eyes.

"You're right," she said. "But what
kind of plan?"

"What about this?" said Mabel,

 and she
whispered in
Holly's ear.
"Yes!" said
Holly. "Let's
do it!"

The next morning, Mabel slipped on
her red dress and raced to school.
Holly was waiting at the school gate.
Arm in arm, they marched into the
playground.

"Here comes that traffic light again," sneered John, pointing at Mabel.

"I love traffic lights," said Mabel.

"Me too," said Holly. "They're pretty and bright."

"What?" said John.

"Well, I think Mabel looks more like
a tomato," said Paul.

"Tomatoes are gorgeous," said Mabel.

"Juicy and sweet," said Holly.

"What?" said Paul.

"Well, Holly looks like a boiled egg,"
said Emma.

"Boiled eggs are delicious,"
said Holly.

"They're good for you, too,"
said Mabel.

"What?" said Emma.

"You two are crazy," said John.

"Crazy is fun!" said Mabel and Holly, joining hands and dancing around.

John didn't know what to say next.

Neither did Paul.

Neither did Emma.

They were speechless.

"Come on, Holly," said Mabel.

"Let's get away from these three — they're boring!"

"Goodbye!" called Mabel and Holly, laughing and running off.

The school bell rang.

"You know, John is right," said Mabel. "We really *are* crazy."

"What?" said Holly.

"Well, I'm crazy about your beautiful haircut," said Mabel.

Holly smiled. "And I'm crazy about your beautiful red dress."

Then, hand in hand, Mabel and Holly skipped happily into the classroom.

About the Author and Illustrator

Frieda Wishinsky grew up in New York City. She has always loved to tell stories, and has written many books for children, often inspired by her own life. Frieda says, "Just like Mabel, I love red. And just like Mabel, I didn't like my name when I was younger – but now I don't mind it at all!" Frieda now lives with her family in Toronto, Canada.

Sue Heap has written and illustrated many books for children, and in 1998 she won the Smarties Prize – the UK's biggest book award. Sue had fun inventing all Mabel's different clothes. She says, "Mabel's such a sparky character I knew she had to have a wardrobe to match!" Sue's other books for Kingfisher include the picture book, *Baby Bill and Little Lill*.

Tips for Beginner Readers

1. Think about the cover and the title of the book. What do you think it will be about? While you are reading, think about what might happen next and why.

2. As you read, ask yourself if what you're reading makes sense. If it doesn't, try rereading or look at the pictures for clues.

3. If there is a word that you do not know, look carefully at the letters, sounds, and word parts that you do know. Blend the sounds to read the word. Is this a word you know? Does it make sense in the sentence?

4. Think about the characters, where the story takes place, and the problems the characters in the story faced. What are the important ideas in the beginning, middle and end of the story?

5. Ask yourself questions like:
Did you like the story?
Why or why not?
How did the author make it fun to read?
How well did you understand it?

Maybe you can understand the story better if you read it again!